To Grandma Laura and Aunt Agnes.
Steadfast allies and loving adversaries forever.

—M. P.

Library of Congress Cataloging-in-Publication Data
Player, Micah.
Chloe, instead / by Micah Player.
p. cm.
Summary: Chloe is not what her older sister expected,
but maybe that is just what makes her special and lovable.
ISBN 978-0-8118-7865-4 (alk. paper)
1. Sisters—Juvenile fiction. 2. Individuality in children—Juvenile fiction.
[1. Sisters—Fiction. 2. Individuality—Fiction.] I. Title.
PZ7.P71385Ch 2012
813.54—dc22
2011012717

Book design by Mai Ogiya.
Typeset in Martin Gothic.
The illustrations in this book were rendered digitally then finished with india ink and watercolor.

Manufactured in China, April 2012.

10 9 8 7 6 5 4 3 2

Chronicle Books LLC
680 Second Street, San Francisco, California 94107

www.chroniclekids.com

Chloe, instead

by micah player

chronicle books · san francisco

This is **my** house.

At least,
it used to be.

Now, it's **our** house.

I was hoping for
a little sister who was
just like me.

But I got **Chloe,** instead.

She's **nothing** like me.

I color with crayons.

Chloe thinks they're delicious.

I love books.

So does Chloe.

She can't get enough of them.

Actually, Chloe can't seem to get enough of **anything**.

Especially **my** things.

Go away,
Chloe!

I need to practice.

Come back. I'm sorry, Chloe.

Do you want to dance?

(Chloe loves to dance.)

Dance, Chloe!

This used to be **my** house.

Now, it's **our** house.

I'm glad I didn't get a little sister
who was just like me.

Because I got **Chloe** . . .

instead.